MY GRIEF COMFORT BOOK

Creative Activities to Help Kids Cope with Loss and Keep Memories Alive

Brie Overton

Illustrated by Jesse White

Storey Publishing

The mission of Storey Publishing is to serve our customers by publishing practical information that encourages personal independence in harmony with the environment.

Edited by Deanna F. Cook
Art direction and book design
 by Jessica Armstrong
Text production by Jennifer Jepson Smith
Illustrations by © Jesse White

Text © 2025 by Brianne L. Overton

All rights reserved. Hachette Book Group supports the right to free expression and the value of copyright. The purpose of copyright is to encourage writers and artists to produce the creative works that enrich our culture. The scanning, uploading, and distribution of this book without permission is a theft of the author's intellectual property. If you would like permission to use material from the book (other than for review purposes), please contact permissions@hbgusa.com. Thank you for your support of the author's rights.

 The information in this book is true and complete to the best of our knowledge. All recommendations are made without guarantee on the part of the author or Storey Publishing. The author and publisher disclaim any liability in connection with the use of this information.

 The publisher is not responsible for websites (or their content) that are not owned by the publisher.

 Storey books may be purchased in bulk for business, educational, or promotional use. Special editions or book excerpts can also be created to specification. For details, please contact your local bookseller or the Hachette Book Group Special Markets Department at special.markets@hbgusa.com.

Storey Publishing
210 MASS MoCA Way
North Adams, MA 01247
storey.com

Storey Publishing is an imprint of Workman Publishing, a division of Hachette Book Group, Inc., 1290 Avenue of the Americas, New York, NY 10104. The Storey Publishing name and logo are registered trademarks of Hachette Book Group, Inc.

Distributed in Europe by Hachette Livre, 58 rue Jean Bleuzen, 92 178 Vanves Cedex, France
Distributed in the United Kingdom by Hachette Book Group, UK, Carmelite House, 50 Victoria Embankment, London EC4Y 0DZ

ISBNs: 978-1-63586-822-7 (paperback with 8 perforated text sheets, 4 perforated cardstock sheets, and 2 sticker sheets); 978-1-63586-782-4 (fixed format EPUB); 978-1-63586-932-3 (fixed format PDF); 978-1-63586-933-0 (fixed format Kindle)

Printed in Humen Town, Dongguan, China by R. R. Donnelley on paper from responsible sources
10 9 8 7 6 5 4 3 2 1

APS

**To my tyke and teen who inspire me daily.
And to all my campers and kiddos—
your ability to grow through your grief
is as brave as you.**

Acknowledgments

I've had the wonderful opportunity to work with many organizations, schools, bereavement centers, and hospice groups throughout my career. The following activities are a compilation of the amazing work we've created together as we served grieving children, teenagers, and adults.

CONTENTS

Hello and Welcome 7

Activities for saying goodbye:

Before and After Drawings 8

Goodbye Letter 10

Comfort Kit 12

A Secret Spot 15

Roller Coaster 16

A Story to Remember 19

Poetry Word Scramble 21

Projects for letting out feelings:

What's in My Heart? 22

Tangled Ball of Grief 24

Inside-Outside Mask 26

Scream Box 28

Paper-Bag Piñata 30

Wash Away Worries 32

Finger-Painted Feelings 34

Grief X-ray 36

Smash Your Anger 38

Memory-making crafts:

Memory Quilt 40

Wind Chimes of Remembrance 42

Scrapbook of You 44

Memory Bracelet 46

Cook a Favorite Recipe 48

My Memory Box 50

Adventure Jar 52

Memory Stones 55

Light a Candle 56

My Place for You 58

Special Touches 60

HELLO AND WELCOME

I am so glad this book found you. I hope it will be a comforting way to work through your feelings after someone you cared about died. Whether you have lost a parent, a pet, an aunt or uncle, or another special person in your life, it's normal to experience grief.

Grief is what we feel when someone we care about dies. You may be sad, lonely, hurt, angry, worried, happy, or upset. All of these emotions are part of grief, and all of them are welcome. There is no right or wrong way to grieve, and you will experience your own unique grief journey.

The activities in this book will help you work through your feelings of loss to find comfort and peace. It can be healing to draw a picture, write a letter, make a wind chime, or tell a good story about someone you miss.

Share these activities with your family and friends. Grieving together helps us to connect and care for one another. It also helps us remember the special people we love and miss.

BRIE OVERTON

Bonus: Turn to page 60 to find stationery, poetry cards, stickers, and more to help you complete the activities in this book.

BEFORE AND AFTER DRAWINGS

Big changes happen when someone you care about dies. Drawing can be helpful. Take some time to tell your story in pictures.

Before

- Gather colored pencils, crayons, or markers and two sheets of paper.

- On one piece of paper, draw a picture of a day before your person died.

- As you draw, think about what life was like before your person died.

- What do you remember? What do you miss?

After

- On the second sheet of paper, draw a picture of today. Show what your life is like now, after your person died.

- Look at the two pictures side by side.

- What makes your life different? What changes happened? Did anything stay the same?

GOODBYE LETTER

Writing a letter can help you say goodbye to someone you've lost. You can tell them what they meant to you and thank them for being in your life. You can also give them an update on your life now.

- Grab a pen or pencil. Take out the Goodbye Letter Stationery on page 61.

- Think about what you want to say in your letter.

- Write about how you feel. What do you miss about your special person?

- Thank them for something they did or said that you feel grateful for.

- Include anything you didn't get the chance to say before they died.

- Fold up your letter and write your person's name on the other side. Add the Goodbye Letter Seal and Goodbye Letter Stamp stickers from page 87.

- You can open and read the letter to help you feel connected, or share it with someone you trust.

COMFORT KIT

Some days, you may need a little extra comfort. Make a kit for yourself by filling a small box with things that help you feel calmer. These should be items you can touch, smell, hear, and taste.

Put the items below in a small box:

- A favorite book to read
- Soft or fuzzy fabric
- Comfort Cards from page 77
- Peppermint candy or a scented marker
- A jingling bell
- A photo that makes you happy
- A mug for a hot drink
- Tissues for tears

Use My Stickers from pages 85 and 87 to decorate your box.

Settle in with your kit:

- Read the Comfort Cards or your favorite book.

- Jingle the bell and listen.

- Smell the calming scent of the peppermint candy.

- Rub the soft fabric between your fingers.

- Enjoy a warm drink in the mug.

A SECRET SPOT

Create a comfy place just for you in a corner of your home. This secret spot will give you room to think and a safe space to grieve.

- Imagine a cozy fort you would like to hide in. Maybe it's a spaceship, a bird's nest, or a tent.

- Grab paper and crayons or markers. Draw your dream space.

- Try building it in the corner of a room. You can use sheets and blankets held together with clothespins, pillows leaned on chairs, decorated cardboard, or painted poster board taped together.

- Put cozy pillows and blankets inside.

- Now climb into your hideaway and dream.

IT'S OKAY TO REST

ROLLER COASTER

Have you ever been on a roller coaster? There are ups and downs, twists and turns, loops and hills, and highs and lows. Losing someone can feel like being on a roller coaster, too.

- Draw a roller coaster of your journey since your person passed away.

- Add words to your picture to describe the ups and downs, twists and turns, and highs and lows.

A STORY TO REMEMBER

Here's a storytelling activity to get you talking about your special person. Do this with a friend or family member who knew your special person.

- Put all the A Story to Remember Cards on page 63 into a basket.

- Pick one card and read it aloud.

- Finish the sentence on the card using memories of your special person, and let the words help you tell a story.

- Take turns picking cards and telling stories.

- You might be surprised at how many stories pop into your head!

POETRY WORD SCRAMBLE

Writing a poem can help you express your feelings. But sometimes it's hard to find the words to write. Try this activity to inspire a poem.

- Take out the **Poetry Scramble Words on pages 65 and 66**.

- Lay the words on the floor or a table.

- Choose the words you want to use. Put them next to each other to create a short poem.

WHAT'S IN MY HEART?

Who are the people you care about most? What do you love? Show what you hold close to your heart with this drawing activity.

- Take out the What's in My Heart activity sheet on page 67.

- Use crayons or markers to fill in your heart with drawings.

- Sketch pictures of people and pets you love.

- Add memories and symbols of anything that's special to you!

TANGLED BALL OF GRIEF

Are you feeling happy or sad, angry or glad? Or all these feelings at the same time? Sometimes our emotions get tangled up together. It is okay to feel what you feel.

- Find the My Tangled Ball activity sheet on page 69.

- Think about the emotions you feel right now. Are you sad, calm, happy, or scared?

- Choose a colored marker or crayon for each emotion you feel, such as yellow for happy or black for scared. Scribble each color around and around the ball.

- Fill your ball with scribbles of all the emotions you feel right now.

INSIDE-OUTSIDE MASK

Sometimes our face looks different than how we feel on the inside. Color a mask to show both sides of your wonderful self.

Outside

- Remove the Inside-Outside Mask on page 79.

- On one side, use colored pencils or markers to draw what people see when they look at you.

- What does your expression look like? What do you share about yourself?

Inside

- On the other side of the mask, draw what you are feeling on the inside.

- What do you hide from others?

- What do you keep inside?

- Tape a popsicle stick or pencil to the bottom of the mask.

- Share both sides with someone you trust.

THERE ARE MANY SIDES OF ME

SCREAM BOX

Have you ever wanted to scream but held it in? Letting yourself express strong emotions is healthy. Holding back can be harmful to your body and mind. Practice letting it all out with this Scream Box.

1. Stuff a cardboard box and a paper-towel tube with newspaper or tissue paper.

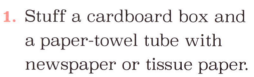

2. Poke the paper-towel tube into the box opening. Leave the top of the paper-towel tube sticking out. Tape the box closed around the tube.

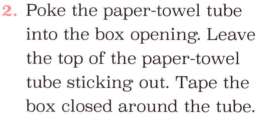

3. Use markers or crayons and My Stickers on pages 85 and 87 to decorate your tube and box.

4. Now count down: *3 . . . 2 . . . 1 . . . SCREAM* (into the tube)! The paper will absorb the sound of your scream.

PAPER-BAG PIÑATA

Fill a paper piñata with your thoughts written on tiny slips of paper. Then tear it apart to let the feelings go free!

1. Pick a word that describes how you are feeling from the Paper-Bag Piñata Words on page 71. Or write whatever makes you angry, upset, or frustrated on the blank slips.

2. Put the strips in a paper bag. The bag represents you.

3. Add candy to the bag and staple it shut. The candies are the sweet things inside you that help you cope with hard feelings.

4. Tape or glue strips of tissue paper or streamers on the outside of the paper bag.

5. Hold the bag up high and tear it open. Let the words and candy fall all around you.

I AM LEARNING TO FIND JOY AGAIN

WASH AWAY WORRIES

Erase your worries with some water-filled balloons!

1. Use chalk to write your worries on a sidewalk, driveway, or brick wall outside.

2. Fill up several balloons with water. Knot them.

3. Take a couple of deep breaths.

4. Now throw the water balloons at your chalk worries.

5. Watch the balloons pop and the words disappear.

LET THE BALLOONS HELP WASH YOUR WORRIES AWAY . . .

FINGER-PAINTED FEELINGS

Grief can be messy—and so can finger painting. You may feel bright or dark, loud or quiet, and even big or small. Touch the paint and let your fingers tell the story of your grief.

1. Gather finger paint and a big piece of paper.

2. Dip your hands in the paint. You can use different colors to show a mix of emotions.

3. Spread the paint all over the paper. As you swirl the paint, think about how you are feeling.

4. What does it feel like to make art with your hands? What does your painting look like?

EVERYONE'S GRIEF LOOKS A LITTLE DIFFERENT

GRIEF X-RAY

Grief often weighs us down with sadness, and we can feel it inside our bodies. Think about where you carry your grief. Maybe you feel heavy in your shoulders or foggy in your head. Can you draw an X-ray of it?

- Tear out the Grief X-ray activity sheet on page 73.

- Use markers or crayons to show your feelings on the inside.

- Think about these questions to help you draw:

    * Are your shoulders heavy like a bag of rocks?

    * Do your insides feel gray like a rainy day?

    * Does your chest feel tight like a rubber band is wrapped around it?

    * Do your feet feel cold like blocks of ice?

I FEEL MY GRIEF AND THEN I LET IT GO

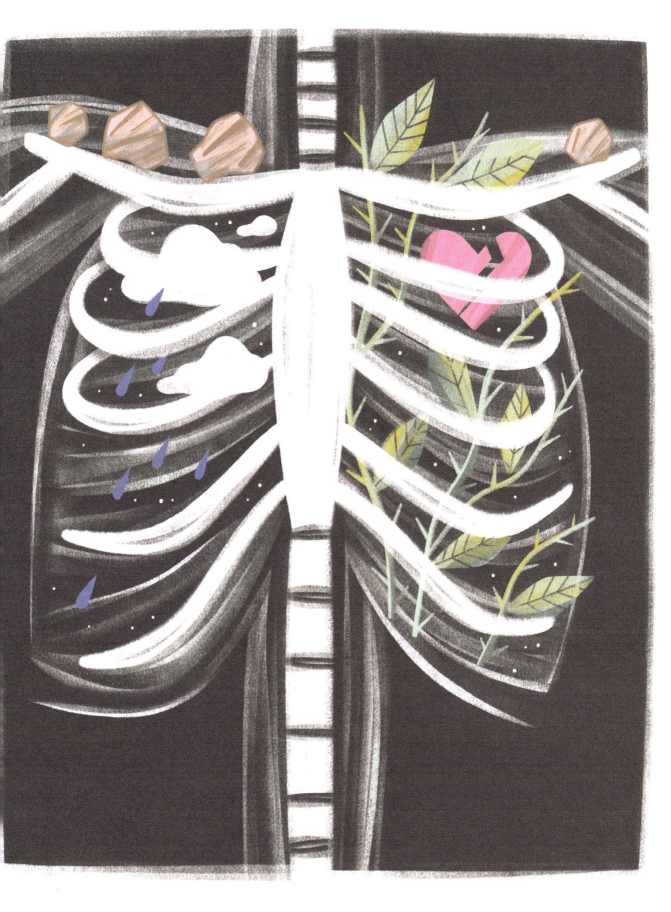

SMASH YOUR ANGER

If you're angry, it might feel good to smash something like an old garden pot, plate, or mug that no one uses anymore. Decorate it with words that describe what you're mad about. Then smash it to pieces!

1. Gather markers and a small terra-cotta pot (or an old ceramic plate or mug).

2. What words come to mind when you are angry? *Mad*? *Hot*? *Furious*? Write them on the pot (or plate or mug).

3. Put the pot in a plastic bag and seal it. Cover it with a second plastic bag and seal it, too, so the broken pieces won't fly everywhere.

4. Ask an adult for help. Grab a small hammer. Now count down: *5 . . . 4 . . . 3 . . . 2 . . . 1 . . . SMASH*!

5. How did it feel? What words can you see in the smashed pot?

MEMORY QUILT

Make a quilt to celebrate someone special. On squares of fabric or paper, draw a memory or write a word that reminds you of them. Connect the squares to tell a story of the person you loved.

1. Gather pieces of fabric (for example, old T-shirts, quilt squares, an old blanket) or colored paper. Cut the fabric or paper into squares.

2. Think about the person you are remembering today. Who were they? What do you miss about them? What made them special? What did they like to do?

3. Use fabric markers (or permanent markers) to draw or write some favorite memories on the fabric or paper squares.

4. Have a grown-up help you stitch the fabric squares together with needle and thread, or connect them with safety pins. Or tape the paper squares together.

CLOTHING QUILT

Ask a grown-up who sews to help you make a quilt out of your person's old shirts, T-shirts, and jeans.

WIND CHIMES OF REMEMBRANCE

Capture the breeze and the spirit of someone special by making a wind chime. Think about your person as you make the chime. What made them special to you? What do you miss about them? When the wind blows, listen closely and feel the breeze—and your connection.

1. Poke several holes around the rim and one hole in the bottom of a paper cup with a pencil. The cup bottom will be the top of your wind chime.

2. String twine through each rim hole. Leave enough twine to tie a knot on the outside of the cup to keep the twine in place.

3. Decorate each strand of twine. You can use jingle bells, beads, and jewels.

4. Add **My Stickers on pages 85 and 87** to the cup.

5. Hang your wind chime with another piece of twine threaded through the hole at the top, and wait for the wind to blow.

SCRAPBOOK OF YOU

One nice way to remember someone you've lost is by creating a scrapbook. When you are missing your person, you can flip through the pages and smile at their photos, read their jokes, and remember good times together.

1. Gather small pictures of the two of you together, postcards of places you visited, and slips of paper with funny jokes and sayings.

2. Find the Scrapbook Cover on page 81. Decorate the cover with your person's name and My Stickers on pages 85 and 87.

3. Place the cover on top of a stack of paper that's the same size. Punch holes in the paper to line up with the cover holes. Tie the scrapbook together with yarn.

I TREASURE AND CELEBRATE YOUR LIFE

4. Tape or glue pictures, postcards, and notes to the pages.

5. Use markers, colored pencils, crayons, and My Stickers from pages 85 and 87 to personalize the pages of your scrapbook.

6. Flip through the scrapbook whenever you miss your person and want to see their smile.

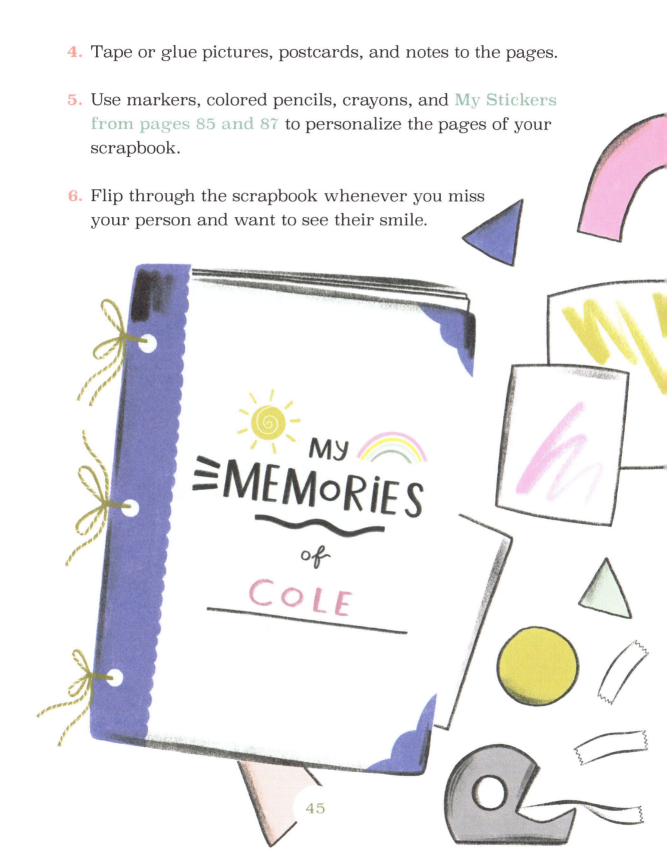

MEMORY BRACELET

Many things can help us remember our person—one of their favorite shirts, a hat they loved, or a necklace they wore. You can also make a bracelet to wear in honor of your person with beads and letters.

1. Choose beads that remind you of your person. You might pick beads in their favorite colors or use the colors of their favorite sports team. Or choose alphabet beads that spell their name.

2. Cut a piece of elastic string longer than what will fit around your wrist. Tie a knot at one end.

3. One by one, slide your beads onto the string.

4. Once you are finished, ask an adult to help you tie the bracelet around your wrist.

SAVE THREE THINGS

When someone dies, their belongings are often given away or donated. Ask a grown-up if you can keep three special things to remember them by.

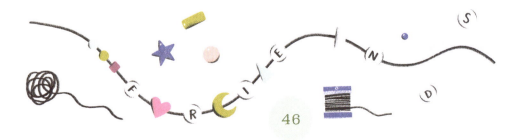

EACH BEAD REMINDS ME OF YOU

COOK A FAVORITE RECIPE

What was your special person's favorite food? Invite friends over to enjoy it with you, and share stories that make you smile.

- What did your special person love to eat?

- Is there a recipe the two of you enjoyed cooking together?

- Is there something they used to make that you really enjoyed, like chocolate-chip cookies or lasagna?

- With the help of an adult, make one of these recipes.

- Invite family or friends over to enjoy it with you. Share stories, memories, and laughs as you eat the delicious food together.

SAVE THE RECIPE

After you make the recipe, write it on one of the Recipe Cards on page 83. Then put it in Scrapbook of You (see page 44) or My Memory Box (see page 50). You can make the recipe again on their birthday or any time you want to connect with them.

MY MEMORY BOX

You probably have pictures, keepsakes, and cards that remind you of your special person. Create a place where you can keep them all together. Whenever you want to spend some time thinking about your person, pull out your box and explore your keepsakes.

- Find a box (a shoebox or similar-size container) to hold your memories.

- Fill the box with letters, pictures, cards, and things that remind you of your person.

- Add a pad of paper so you can write or draw memories each time you open your box.

- Decorate the outside of the box with My Stickers from pages 85 and 87. Write your person's name on the box in special letters.

- Sort through your box whenever you are missing your person, and remember why they were so loved.

ADVENTURE JAR

What did your person love to do when they were alive? Did they enjoy bowling, hiking, traveling, exploring museums, trying new foods, or going to shows? Add all these activities to your adventure jar. It will hold many opportunities to try something new.

1. Choose some activities from My Adventure Jar activity sheet on page 75 that your person loved. Write down any other activities they enjoyed doing on the blank slips.

2. Tear out each piece of paper, fold it, and put it in a jar.

3. Decorate your jar with My Stickers from pages 85 and 87.

4. Ready for an adventure? Pick a slip of paper from your jar. With a grown-up's permission or help, give that activity a try. You'll learn new things about yourself, discover hidden talents, and honor your special person with each adventure.

MEMORY STONES

Decorate stones to honor someone special. You can place the stones anywhere to remember your person. Try putting one outside a door where you live, and each time you come home, you can think of them.

1. Gather several small, flat stones. Wipe them off to remove any dirt.

2. Decorate them with the Memory Stone Stickers on page 87, or paint them.

3. Find a special place to put the stones where you will see them and remember your person. You can put them outside or inside—wherever you are often passing by. You may choose to place them in a park or along your favorite walking path for others to see.

PLANT A TREE

Ask a grown-up to help you plant a tree in honor of your loved one. Leave your stones beneath it. And watch it grow over the years.

LIGHT A CANDLE:

Celebrate your person's birthday, their death date, or another important day in their life by quietly watching a candle's flame.

- Find a candle in their favorite color or in a scent they loved.

- With a grown-up's permission, carefully light the candle.

- Look at the flame and think about the warmth your special person brought to your life.

- Read the poem below aloud.

- Ask friends and family members who live far away to all light a remembrance candle at the same time.

This candle helps me remember

All the good times we shared together.

I watch the light flicker and shine,

And I'm so thankful we had our time.

MY PLACE FOR YOU

Set up a memory space on a mantel or shelf to honor people and pets who have died. When you walk by this space, you can say hello to their pictures or tell them about your day.

- Put framed photos of relatives, pets, and others you deeply miss on a shelf.

- Add a candle, a potted plant or flowers, trinkets, jewelry, or other mementos that remind you of your special people or pets.

- The memory space can be a place for you to honor those you've lost and to feel grateful for the time you had together.

YOU ARE FOREVER LOVED

SPECIAL TOUCHES

On the following pages you'll find activity sheets, cards, and stickers that you can use to complete many of the activities in this book.

Carefully remove the pages from the book along the dotted lines.

Be sure to read the directions for each activity in the main part of the book before you get started.

GOODBYE LETTER STATIONERY

GOODBYE LETTER STATIONERY

To _____

From _____

A STORY TO REMEMBER CARDS

Remember when we . . .	You loved to eat . . .
You used to call me . . .	One holiday, you . . .
I learned from you . . .	Good advice you gave me was . . .
I miss your . . .	Once, you told me a funny story about . . .
My earliest memory of you is . . .	My world is different now because . . .
I wish I could tell you . . .	A silly thing you did was . . .

A STORY TO REMEMBER CARDS

POETRY SCRAMBLE WORDS

day	go	talk	fear	for	water
is	kindness	son	believe	a	the
smiles	us	new	broken	music	balance
friends	laugh	is	care	peace	summer
simple	follow	died	grandma	circle	hands
you	life	cousin	black	the	without
dad	where	bridge	game	blue	tear
me	proud	uncle	support	spring	accident
than	yesterday	are	daughter	how	their
hold	eyes	aunt	picture	now	cloud

POETRY SCRAMBLE WORDS

make	hospital	brother	house	brave	white
the	rain	shield	fall	cry	eyes
orange	mom	there	over	lonely	worry
fear	gray	grandpa	shoe	window	car
sister	why	they	sounds	read	baby
grass	is	brave	look	road	stare
think	find	loss	tree	love	play
listen	eat	pool	darkness	stairs	red
real	tomorrow	cup	phone	paper	shift
think	winter	smile	is	light	hope

WHAT'S IN MY HEART

Fill in your heart with drawings of people, memories, and anything special to you.

MY TANGLED BALL

Choose a colored marker or crayon for each emotion you feel, such as yellow for happy or black for scared. Scribble each color around and around the ball.

Here are some examples of emotions and colors.

Purple = Mad

Yellow = Happy

Black = Scared

Blue = Sad

Green = Calm

Pink = Loved

MY TANGLED BALL

Choose a colored marker or crayon for each emotion you feel, such as yellow for happy or black for scared. Scribble each color around and around the ball.

Here are some examples of emotions and colors.

Purple = Mad   **Yellow = Happy**   **Black = Scared**   **Blue = Sad**   **Green = Calm**   **Pink = Loved**

PAPER-BAG PIÑATA WORDS

Choose the words below that represent your emotions and feelings.
Write your own words on the blank slips. Add them to your piñata.

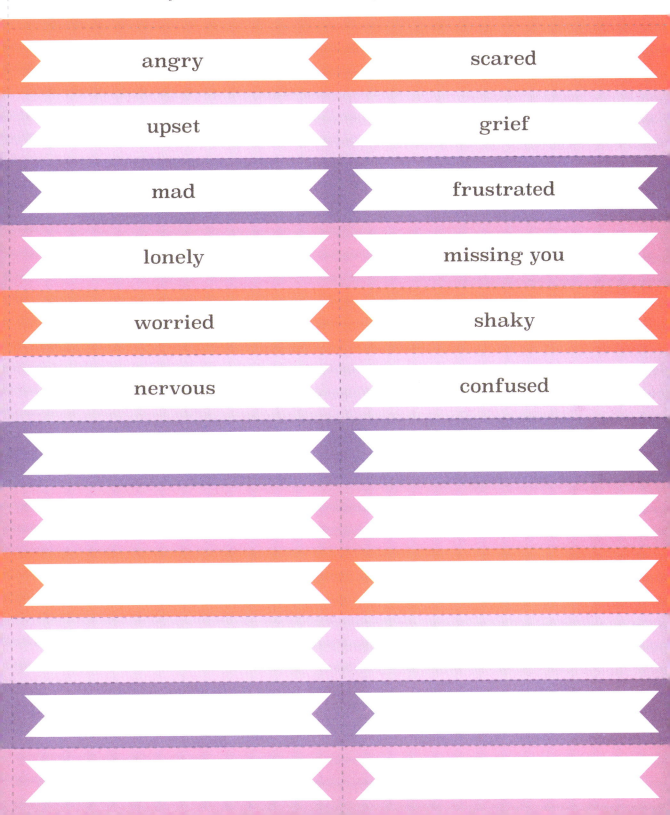

- angry
- scared
- upset
- grief
- mad
- frustrated
- lonely
- missing you
- worried
- shaky
- nervous
- confused

PAPER-BAG PIÑATA WORDS

GRIEF X-RAY

Draw where you feel grief in your body.

GRIEF X-RAY

Draw where you feel grief in your body.

MY ADVENTURE JAR

Choose the activities below that your person loved. Write down other activities they enjoyed doing on the blank slips. Put them in your adventure jar.

Play a game	Go to a park
Listen to music	Visit a museum
Make a recipe	Take a walk
Take a ride to _____	Tell a joke
Read a book	Watch a show

MY ADVENTURE JAR

COMFORT CARDS

COMFORT CARDS

INSIDE-OUTSIDE MASK

THIS is HOW I LOOK on the OUTSIDE

INSIDE-OUTSIDE MASK

THIS is WHAT I FEEL on the INSIDE

MY MEMORIES

of

_____

RECIPE

NAME

INGREDIENTS

RECIPE

NAME

INGREDIENTS

RECIPE CARDS

RECIPE

DIRECTIONS

RECIPE

DIRECTIONS